CANARY ACROSS THE MERSEY

This book is based on the real life experiences of the author as a young boy and dedicated to his parents, Lily and Roy Boyle, and class teacher, Mrs Rose Purcell.

Canary Across the Mersey

Written by Dr Michael Boyle

Illustrated by Ian Wright

Michael was a typical nine year old boy, full of energy and curiosity. He had brown hair and blue eyes and enjoyed playing football in the school yard with his friends.

He went to school at St. George's Juniors near Liverpool. The school sat between a lovely old church and an apple orchard.

The birds sang in the trees, and a little donkey spent his time swishing his tail as he ate the fallen juicy-ripe apples.

It was while Michael was playing football one day that out of the corner of his eye he saw something fluttering. He turned, and then saw a bright yellow bird had just landed on the school wall.

"Wowzer, that's not a sparrow, it's a canary," he exclaimed. Michael wondered how he could catch the little yellow bird because he knew it would not survive for long in the wild.

That evening he told his mother about the canary. She said to him, "There is an old bird cage in the attic that you could take to school. Put some seed inside and see if the canary will go in."

The next day he left the cage near the wall where he had seen the bird, and went inside for his lessons. When he returned to the cage there was the canary sitting on the perch.

Michael was so excited. He closed the cage door and took the canary inside to Mrs Purcell his class teacher, who agreed to let the canary become the class pet.

Michael and the canary were both very popular at school, and the children took it in turns to take the canary home for the weekend.

Life at school could not have been better.

A big yard to play football and dream of becoming a footballer; an apple orchard next door and a derelict old house that Michael and his friends pretended was haunted. And of course, Mrs Purcell, Michael's class teacher...

... What could go wrong?

Michael was quite an inquisitive boy who enjoyed reading. He liked the Liverpool Echo newspaper, especially the pink football edition on a Saturday night.

Lying on the carpet he had the newspaper open at the 'Lost and Found' page. His eye caught sight of an advert and he said...

"... Mum, listen to this, '**LOST** - yellow canary, answers to the name of Peter. **Reward if found**,' I wonder if this is our canary?"

On the advert there was a phone number to ring.
Michael's dad recognised that the number was from the Wirral on the other side of the River Mersey.

Michael's mum decided to call the number. A polite old lady answered the phone and Michael listened anxiously, as his mum recounted the tale of saving the canary in the school playground and adopting it as the class pet.

The old lady on the phone asked Michael's mum if she could put the phone next to the cage so that she could speak to the bird. The lady had a sister, and between them they whistled and talked and then declared, "That's our canary, he knows it is us."

'Good grief,' thought Michael, "this is impossible," but his mum and dad, being the kind people they were, invited the two sisters to their house to confirm the canary was truly theirs.

The two sisters came the very next day and both agreed beyond doubt that indeed this was their canary.
"It must have flown all the way across the River Mersey," one of the sisters said.

Michael looked very sad as he waved goodbye to the canary, who was in the back seat of the sisters' car. He thought "Why did I ever read the Lost and Found column in the Echo newspaper?"

Michael wondered how did the canary cross the River Mersey?

Was it through a Tunnel?

Was it in a yellow submarine?

Or did he cross on the Royal Iris ferry?

Did he swim across the river?

Or did he catch a lift on a hot air balloon?

And then did he fly between the Liver Birds?

Michael's mum and dad realised that by doing the right thing in returning the canary to his owners, they had somehow let Michael down.

In order to make everyone happy, mum went to the local pet shop and bought a blue budgie for the class.

The children named the budgie '**Bluey Boyle**' and it quickly became the star of the class. The children never forgot the canary and are still wondering how did he cross the River Mersey...

... was it through the Mersey tunnel or in a yellow submarine? Did he catch the Royal Iris ferry or swim with the fish? Or did he catch a lift on a hot air balloon and then did he fly between the Liver Birds?

Only the canary knows... what do you think?

Maghull
Aintree
Bootle
Goodison Park
Anfield
Everton
Kingsway
Tunnel
Entrance
Queensway
Tunnel Entrance
Ferry
Kingsway Tunnel
Entrance
LIVERPOOL
Albert
Dock
Ferry
Queensway Tunnel
Entrance
The WIRRAL
River Mersey
Birkenhead